Fani Marceau

Joëlle Jolivet

IN THIS BOOK

chronicle books · san francisco

I am in the poppy, said the bee.

I am in the hair, said the barrette.

I am in the nest, said the bird.

I am in the sky, said the cloud.

I am in the tree, said the monkey.

I am in the web, said the spider.

I am in the apricot, said the pit.

I am in the bed, said the teddy bear.

I am in the bus, said the driver.

I am in the lighthouse, said the lighthouse keeper.

I am in the bath, said the child.

I am in the glove, said the hand.

I am in the tunnel, said the train.

I am in the forest, said the mushroom.

I am in the fireplace, said the fire.

I am in the sand, said the scorpion.

I am in the bed, said the dog.

I am in the dark, said the child.

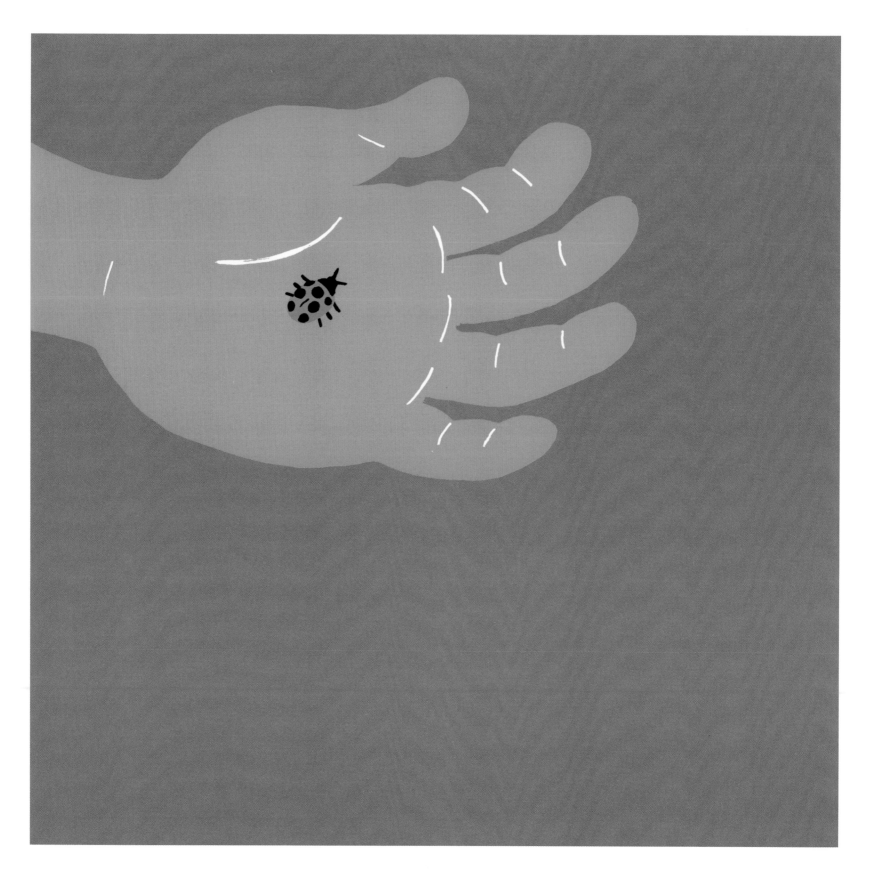

I am in the hand, said the ladybug.

I am in the bowl, said the goldfish.

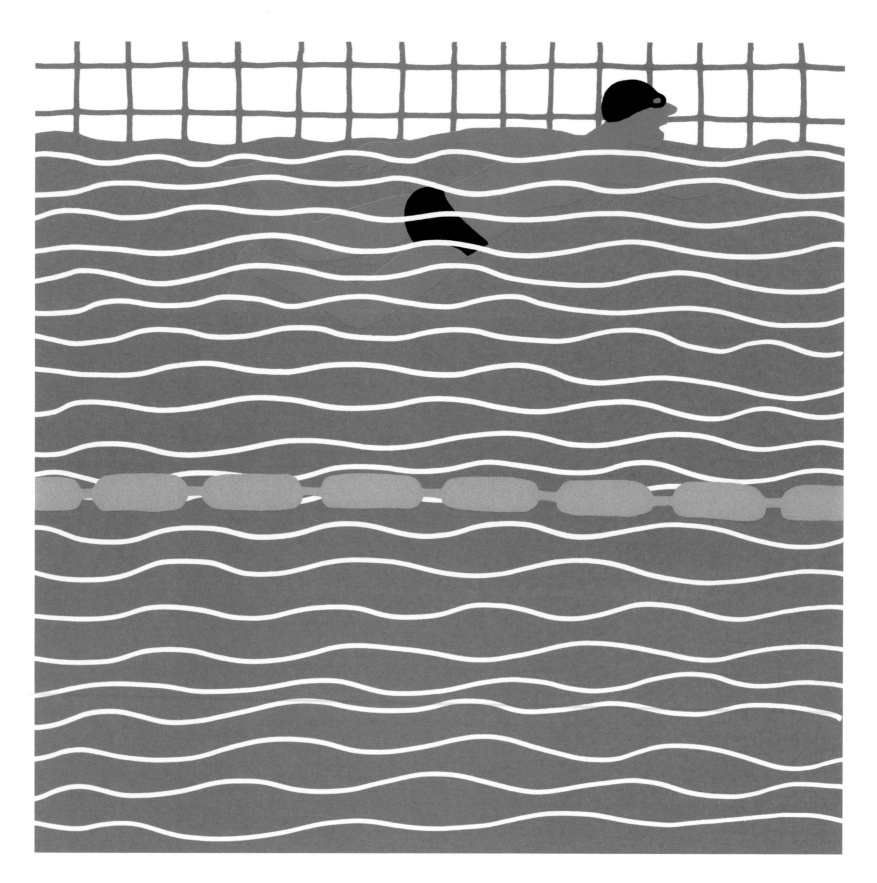

I am in the water, said the swimmer.

I am in the forest, said the wolf.

I am in the train, said the traveller.

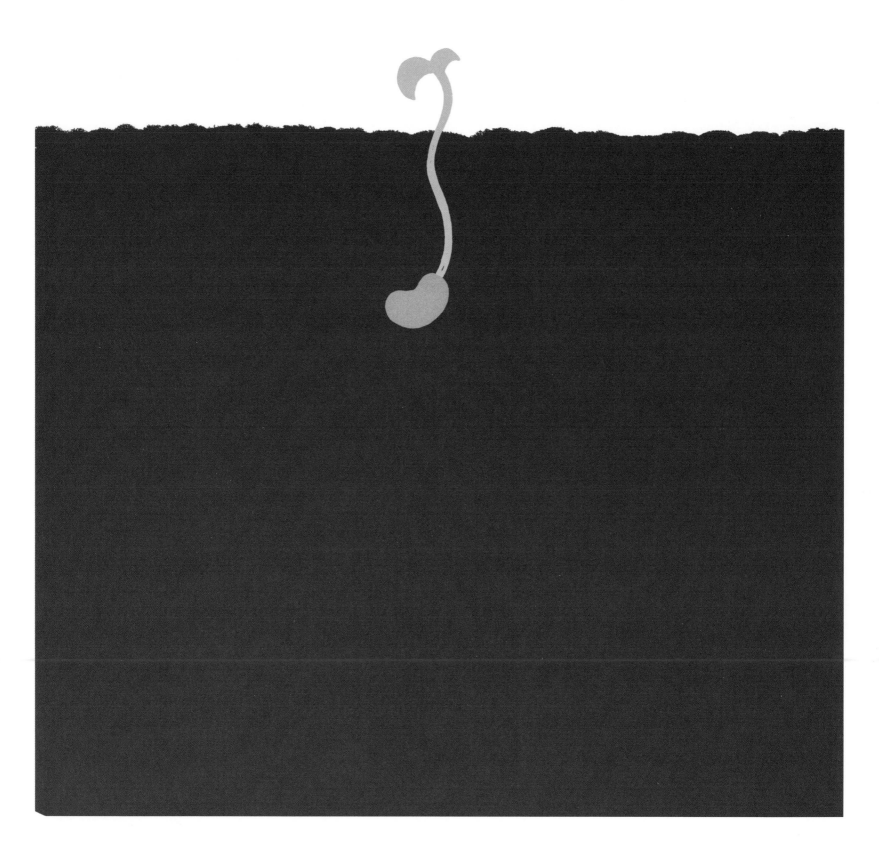

I am in the ground, said the seed.

I am in the stroller, said the child.

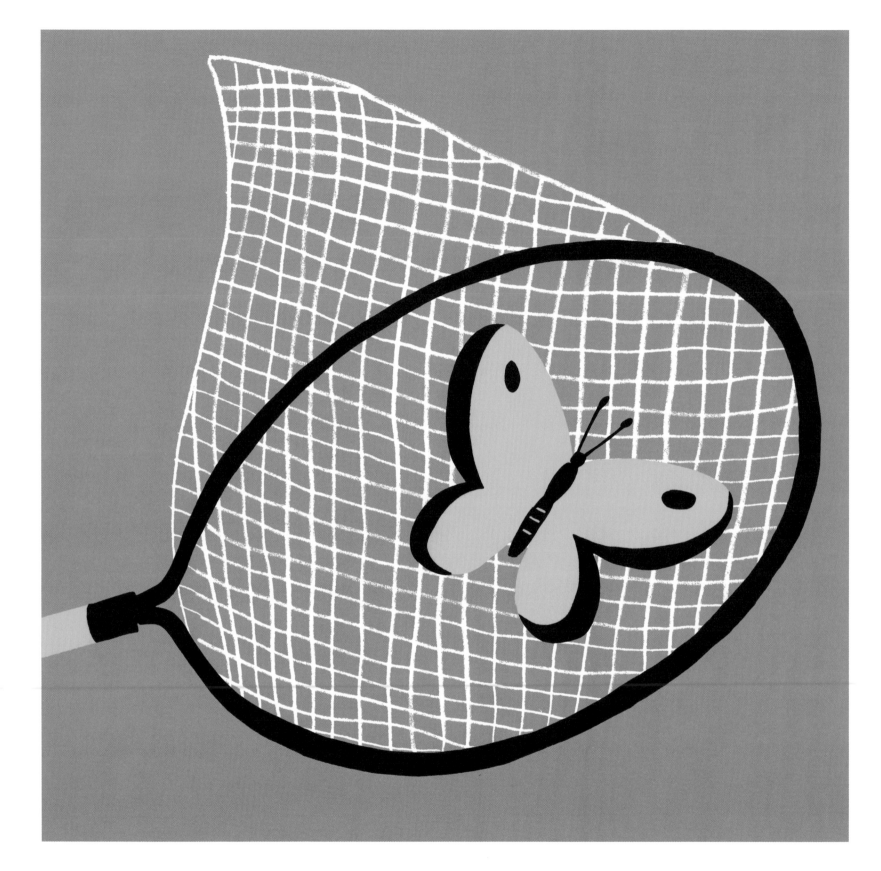

I am in the net, said the butterfly.

I am in space, said the planet.

I am in the jungle, said the tiger.

I am in the garden, said the gardener.

I am in the shoe, said the pebble.

I am in the shell, said the snail.

I am in the field, said the tractor.

I am in the basket, said the salad.

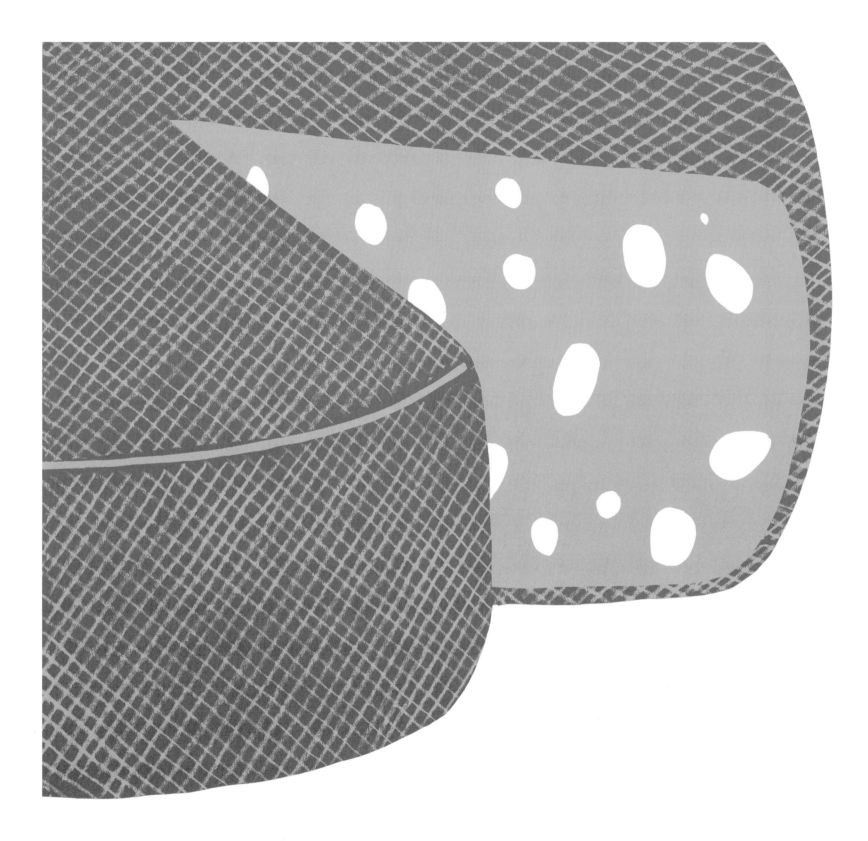

I am in the cheese, said the hole.

I am in the grass, said the ball.

I am in the trunk, said the suitcase.

I am in the borough, said the rabbit.

I am in the chair, said the girl.

I am in the box, said the gift.

I am in the boat, said the sailor.

I am in the ocean, said the whale.

I am in the painting, said the princess.

I am in the herd, said the sheep.

I am in the sand, said the crab.

I am in the mud, said the pig.

I am in the oven, said the meat.

I am in the kitchen, said the chef.

I am in the lock, said the key.

I am in the toolbox, said the hammer.

I am in the shell, said the turtle.

I am in the toy box, said the toy.

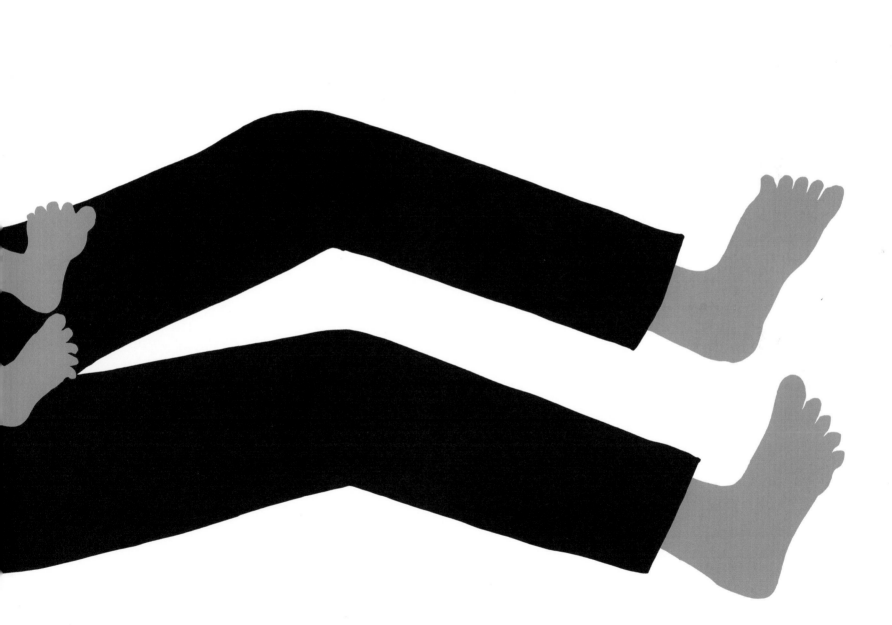

And me, I am in your arms!

E
Marceau,
Fani

First published in the United States of America in 2014 by Chronicle Books LLC.

First published in France in 2012 under the title *Dans le livre*
by hélium, 18 rue Séguier 75006 Paris, France.

Library of Congress Cataloging-in-Publication Data available.

ISBN: 978-1-4521-2588-6

Manufactured in China.

Typeset in Neutra Text Bold Alt and YWFT HLLVTKA.

10 9 8 7 6 5 4 3 2 1

Chronicle Books LLC
680 Second Street
San Francisco, California 94107

Chronicle Books—we see things differently.
Become part of our community at www.chroniclekids.com.